THE SCARECROW HARVEST FESTIVAL

WRITTEN AND ILLUSTRATED BY
JOHN MESZAROS

All rights reserved. No part of this publication may be reproduced, stored in a retrieval system or transmitted, in any form or by any means, electronic, mechanical, photocopying, recording or otherwise, without the prior permission of the copyright holder.

Text and illustrations copyright © 2019 John Meszaros

First Printing July 2019

ISBN: 978-0-578-54309-3

To Isaac

Autumn is here and all the leaves have turned colors, which means the farmers are putting out their scarecrows.

The wind is growing cold and crisp, which means the scarecrows don't want to stay.

Scarecrows are supposed to guard the fields.

Do you know why?

Because the corn is ready to be picked.

Because the apples are ripe and ready for plucking.

And because all the pumpkins are big and orange.

But you know what?

It's hard work guarding those fields,

but the scarecrows don't even get to try that corn,

or those apples,

or those pumpkins

The farmers take it all to the harvest festival.

But you know what else?

The scarecrows don't care.

Because they have their very own...

Scarecrows come from all over for the festival.

They come in all shapes and sizes.

There are scarecrows with heads made from turnips and jack-o-lanterns,

and scarecrows with bodies made from twigs, roots and branches.

There are tiny scarecrows
made from snapdragon flowers and sweetgum balls,

and tiny scarecrows

made from corn husks, teasels and pinecones.

And, of course,
there are scarecrows stuffed with straw.

Scarecrows need to be careful.
If they get caught, the farmers will make them stay to guard the fields.

Scarecrows have many ways to get to the festival.
Some ride bicycles.

Some drive tractors.

Some ride in wagons.

Some fly in balloons
and some ride on broomsticks.

Nothing will keep the scarecrows away from their harvest festival.

Certainly not the farmers.

When they get to the festival there's cider and donuts.

There's grilled corn and apple fritters.

And of course,

there are pumpkins that need to be carved.

Oh wait, it's okay.

It's just a big old skeleton scarecrow!

Phew.

Good thing he made it to the festival.

Wouldn't want to miss this!

It's every scarecrow's favorite time of year!

John Meszaros is an author and artist from Connecticut who always enjoys a good, crisp autumn day with a little bit of spookiness sprinkled in. He loves drawing and writing about monsters, cryptids, yokai and other strange creatures. He also has a soft spot for prehistoric critters and things in the deep sea.

Visit him online at:

www.johnmeszarosart.com

Printed in Great Britain
by Amazon